The ROAR of the CROWD

Also by Rich Wallace

Restless

Losing Is Not an Option

Playing Without the Ball

Shots on Goal

Wrestling Sturbridge

Winning Season Series

Technical Foul

WINNING SEASON

the ROAR of the CROWD

RICH WALLACE

VIKING

VIKING

Published by Penguin Group

Penguin Young Readers Group, 345 Hudson Street, New York, New York 10014, U.S.A.

Penguin Group (Canada), 10 Alcorn Avenue, Toronto, Ontario, Canada M4V 3B2

(a division of Pearson Penguin Canada Inc.)

Penguin Books Ltd, 80 Strand, London WC2R 0RL, England

Penguin Ireland, 25 St Stephen's Green, Dublin 2, Ireland (a division of Penguin Books Ltd)

Penguin Group (Australia), 250 Camberwell Road, Camberwell, Victoria 3124, Australia

(a division of Pearson Australia Group Pty Ltd)

Penguin Books India Pvt Ltd, 11 Community Centre, Panchsheel Park, New Delhi - 110 017, India

Penguin Group (NZ), Cnr Airborne and Rosedale Roads, Albany, Auckland, New Zealand

(a division of Pearson New Zealand Ltd)

Penguin Books (South Africa) (Pty) Ltd, 24 Sturdee Avenue, Rosebank, Johannesburg 2196, South Africa

Penguin Books Ltd, Registered Offices: 80 Strand, London WC2R 0RL, England

First published in 2004 by Viking, a division of Penguin Young Readers Group

3 5 7 9 10 8 6 4 2

Text copyright © Rich Wallace, 2004
All rights reserved

LIBRARY OF CONGRESS CATALOGING-IN-PUBLICATION DATA

Wallace, Rich.

The roar of the crowd / by Rich Wallace.

p. cm. — (Winning Season ; #1)

Summary: After years of playing nothing but soccer in Hudson City, New Jersey,
Manny has to work very hard to play on the middle school football team, using
determination, speed, and smarts to make up for being small and inexperienced.

ISBN 0-670-05940-4 (hardcover)

[1. Football—Fiction. 2. Self-confidence—Fiction. 3. Sportsmanship—Fiction.
4. New Jersey—Fiction.] I. Title.

PZ7.W15877Ro 2004

[Fic]—dc22

2004003406

Manufactured in China
Book design by Jim Hoover
Set in Caslon 224 Book

For Evie

· CONTENTS ·

Playing Time

Manny was angry. He shifted his weight from his right knee to his left and balled his hand into a fist, wishing there was something to smack. He bit hard on his plastic mouth guard and looked up at the practice field.

Vinnie DiMarco, the quarterback, was rolling out toward the sideline, running almost straight toward Manny and the other subs. DiMarco straight-armed a tackler and wiggled loose, but big Anthony Martin hauled him down and tackled him hard at the sideline.

"Nice hustle, Anthony," Manny said, leaping to

his feet to avoid getting rolled on. Anthony nodded and gave a yawn that stretched his chubby brown face until his eyes were nearly shut. He looked exhausted after an hour of scrimmaging in the hot August sun.

Manny had spent the hour watching the first-string offense battle the first-string defense. He hadn't been in for even one play. This wasn't why he'd joined the Hudson City Hornets.

Tired football players stood or kneeled near him, their faces sweaty and their jerseys covered with dirt.

Manny expected to play. So what if he weighed only eighty-seven pounds? He was as tough as anybody out there.

Coach Reynolds walked over near Manny and looked at his clipboard. "You three runts," he said, pointing at Manny, Donald, and Rico. "Get in there at the linebacker spots after this next play. Show me what you can do."

About time, Manny thought. He pulled his helmet down over his dark, curly hair and ran in place for a few seconds, then jumped straight up and down a couple of times. He could feel his heart pumping harder. *I'm gonna nail somebody.*

The next play ended in an incomplete pass, and Manny and the other two trotted onto the field. Manny took his place as middle linebacker. He could hear the defensive linemen panting.

The offense had grinded the ball just over the 50-yard line and had come close to breaking a few long gains. Now DiMarco was calling signals, waiting for the snap. The lone running back went in motion and the ends were split wide. Everything indicated that it would be a pass play.

Don't get burned, Manny thought. He took a step back in anticipation of a quick pass over the middle. But DiMarco took the snap and immediately rolled out to his right, toward the far sideline.

A lineman raced toward Manny and threw his shoulder into him, but Manny dodged to the side and took only a glancing blow. DiMarco had crossed the line of scrimmage now and was turning downfield, a line of blockers clearing his path.

Manny was fast and he eluded another blocker

and angled toward the sideline, sensing that he could catch DiMarco about 30 yards downfield if no one else got there first.

All out, Manny told himself. *Show them what you've got.*

He could feel the dirt kicking up behind him as his cleats drove him toward the ball carrier, tasting the sweat that was trickling off his lip. He was gaining on DiMarco now, cutting down the distance as they raced for the goal line.

DiMarco crossed the 20-yard line, then the 10. Manny was inches away, and he dove, snagging DiMarco's shin and holding on tight. They crashed to the dirt and the ball shook loose, rolling out of bounds.

Manny leaped up. He'd saved a touchdown. What would the coaches think of that?

But as he looked around he saw that the coaches' attention was elsewhere. The other players had already started a long, slow lap around the perimeter of the field. No one was even watching.

"Nice tackle," DiMarco said flatly. "Let's go."

"What?" Manny said.

"That's it. Last play. Coach told us in the huddle. We've got five laps to run. Let's go."

"You're kidding me," Manny said. "I got in for *one play*?"

"Tough break, huh?"

Manny stood still as DiMarco jogged off.

One play?

A whistle blew. "Pick up that football, kid," yelled one of the coaches. "Let's see some hustle."

Manny grabbed the football and started to run, his face getting hot with anger. Most of his teammates were half a lap ahead already. Manny ran to the sideline and dropped the football in disgust. Then he took off after the others.

His breath was steady but hard, coming out in short little bursts as he glared ahead and moved faster. Soon he'd passed the stragglers—Anthony and other linemen drained by the scrimmage, and a few lazy backs whose places in the starting lineup were secure.

Manny picked up the pace as he began his second lap, passing DiMarco and some others and taking aim at the leaders. He swung wide to pass a few more in the end zone, then moved into the lead as he headed along the far sideline.

After four laps Manny was well ahead of everyone, and he sprinted the last one at top speed, still seething from his one-play afternoon.

Coach Reynolds was grinning as Manny yanked off his helmet and walked a few yards to catch his breath. "Good running," he said.

"Right," Manny said.

"You ought to run cross-country in high school," the coach said with a laugh.

"Yeah . . . well I ain't *in* high school," Manny said, trying not to let too much venom into his words. "I'm on this team."

The coach nodded. "I'll try to remember that," he said.

"I hope so."

Coach gave him a stare, but then softened his expression. He pointed a finger at Manny. "Don't get smart," he said. "But keep up the hustle. I was watching that last play. There'll be more chances, believe me."

The Discount Bin

Manny stuck his cleats and mouth guard inside his helmet and carried it all by the face mask. "You coming?" he said to his scrawny friend Donald.

"Yeah," Donald said. Donald was still kneeling by the cooler of water, wiped out from the five laps. "Give me a second. I'm not a marathoner like you are."

Manny shrugged. "Small guys like us better be able to run. It's too easy to get knocked out otherwise."

They headed across the practice field toward

the Boulevard. They both lived on the other side of town, a mile walk from the field. Hudson City was small but dense, the side streets lined with old houses on small lots. The Boulevard was loaded with coffee shops and delis and liquor stores.

"We'll stop and get a soda," Manny said.

"You got any money?"

"I've got a couple of dollars."

"I got a quarter in my shoe," Donald said. "It was digging into my foot the whole time we were running."

"You'll survive."

"Yeah," Donald said. "But I'm starving."

"You won't get much for a quarter."

"Yeah, I will. There's always the discount bin."

They ducked into the small grocery store at the corner of the Boulevard and Ninth, across from St. Joseph's Church. They had to turn sideways to get through the doorway because of their shoulder pads and the stacks of cardboard boxes on the sidewalk.

"Ahh," said Manny, shutting his eyes for a second to enjoy the air-conditioned coolness. "What a difference."

They walked up the canned-soup and pasta aisle toward the baked goods section at the back of the store. The aisles were narrow and stacked high.

"Twinkies," Donald said. "I need Twinkies."

They reached the back and Donald started pawing through the discount bin, where items that were turning stale or had ripped packaging were marked down. "No Twinkies," he said. "Nothing good at all."

Donald glanced around, then flicked his eyebrows up at Manny. He gently brought his helmet down on an individual-sized apple pie, pushing until the box was partly flattened and the pie filling was coming through the crust.

"Oh," Donald said in mock surprise. "I didn't see this pie at first. Looks like a bargain to me."

Manny shook his head. Donald grabbed the pie and they hurried up the aisle. Manny slid open the door of the soda cooler and took out a couple of bottles; then they got in line to pay.

"This was in the discount bin," Donald lied to the teenage girl at the register, handing her the pie. "It isn't marked."

The girl looked at the pie for a few seconds, twisted her mouth around, and sighed.

"Shouldn't be more than a quarter," Donald said.

"Sounds about right," she answered, and punched in the sale.

They laughed as they left the store. "You shouldn't do that," Manny said, but he was grinning.

"It was an emergency," Donald said. "I'd faint if I had to walk all the way home without eating."

Manny had been teammates with Donald before, in Little League baseball and on a parish soccer team. Neither had played organized football before this year, but they'd be entering sixth grade in a few days and figured it was about time. Manny was a little surprised they'd made it through the cuts and actually won places on the roster. Now he was wondering if he should have stuck with soccer, where he was sure he'd be playing instead of sitting on the bench.

"That stunk getting in for only one play," Manny said. "Weren't you angry?"

"Sort of," Donald said. "That's the breaks though. Most of these guys have been playing football since third grade. We're new at it."

"Yeah, I guess."

They walked along in silence for a few minutes, sipping their Cokes and looking at the traffic. They could see the New York City skyline down the hill and across the river.

"Coach said we'd be on some of the special teams, like for kickoffs and punts," Donald said.

"When did he say that?"

"He told me before practice. He's going to start working on that tomorrow. Gotta get ready for the game."

Manny perked up. "Really? You sure? He didn't say anything to me."

"Well, he told me."

"Hope he meant me, too," Manny said.

"I'm sure he did."

The season was set to begin on the following

Saturday, just eight days away. Under the lights at the high school stadium.

They'd reached Manny's street. "See you tomorrow," Manny said.

He put his half-empty soda bottle into one of his cleats and held one shoe in each hand. He put his helmet back on his head and began running up the hill toward his house. In his mind he was racing down the field on a kickoff. The roar of the crowd was deafening.

"Don't you ever need a rest?" Donald called.

"Nah," Manny yelled back. "You've got to be in shape to run down those kick-returners."

Speed and Brains

Five-year-old Sal was waiting for Manny, leaping down the two front steps as Manny came up the sidewalk.

"Hi, Manny!" he hollered.

"Hey, squirt."

"Did you do anything great today?" Sal asked his brother, grabbing Manny's helmet and carrying it up to the porch.

"Sure did," Manny said. "I made this touchdown-saving tackle right at the goal line, Sal. You should have seen me."

"You clobbered the guy, Manny?"

"I clobbered him all right. The big-shot quarterback."

"Wow. *You* should be the quarterback, Manny."

Manny laughed. "I'm too quick for that. They need me to run, not pass. What's for dinner, Sal? I'm starving."

"I don't know. Daddy's not home yet."

"Okay. I'll shower."

Manny entered the kitchen and gave his mom a hug.

"You're soaked with sweat," she said. "You must have been working hard."

"I was. What are you making?"

"Fried fish. It'll be ready soon. Now go get cleaned up."

"Cool."

Manny's mom worked as a bank teller. His dad was a driver for a package-delivery company. Dad could get home anytime between six and eight, depending on the workload.

Sal followed Manny upstairs to the bedroom they shared. Sal had Legos and trucks spread all over the floor. "You should clean this up, buddy,"

Manny said. "I don't want to step on a Lego and break my ankle."

"I will. I was playing all afternoon waiting for you. I was trying to build a football stadium. Like the one you'll be playing in. And the Giants."

Manny patted Sal's head and laughed. "I think Giants Stadium is a little bigger than ours," he said. "We play at the high school field."

"You *should* play at Giants Stadium," Sal said. "You could play for the Giants, couldn't you?"

"Maybe if I ran through their legs or something," Manny said. "I'm hardly big enough for the team I'm on."

Dad was home by the time Manny had showered and dressed. Manny hurried down the stairs.

"Hey, sport," Dad said. "What's the word? Sal said you made some big plays today."

"Just one," Manny said. "A touchdown-saving tackle."

"Not bad," Dad said. "We little guys have to use our speed and our brains, right?"

"Right."

Dad had been a soccer player and had done

some amateur boxing. The boys had a framed photo of him on their wall, fighting in the finals of the New Jersey Golden Gloves tournament at age nineteen. The picture showed him landing a powerful jab to his opponent's jaw, but Dad had always made it clear that he'd lost the fight. "I wanted that title," Dad said, "but he was the better fighter and he deserved it. He fought in the Olympic trials a year or so later."

They sat down to eat. "I'm tired," Mom said. "Busy day at work."

"I'm beat, too," Manny said as he dug into the big plate of food. "And hungry."

"Better eat a lot," Sal said. "So you can keep knocking down that quarterback."

"Yeah," Manny said. "And so I can help you build that stadium!"

Special Attention

*T*he ball was snapped, and Manny shifted on his feet, ready to spring. The momentum was to his right, the tailback barreling toward a hole in the line. Manny charged to the spot, intent on making the tackle, his arms open and tense.

He reached for the tailback, but suddenly his legs went out from under him and he was driven back, falling flat as the runner raced past. He tasted dirt as his face mask hit hard.

"Crap," Manny muttered.

"Sorry," said big Anthony Martin, lying under Manny after making the block. Manny's legs were on Anthony's back.

"Some friend," Manny joked.

"No friends on defense," Anthony said with a grin as he shook Manny off of him.

Manny got to his feet and scurried back into position for the next play. He looked around—it was late in the day. How much playing time would he get? The coach hadn't done anything about special teams yet.

The second-string quarterback came jogging onto the field, so Manny figured there'd be at least a few more plays. This guy had a strong arm but not much accuracy, and he couldn't run as fast as DiMarco. He'd probably stick to a short passing game. Good work for the linebackers.

The guy called signals. Manny took a step back. The ball was snapped and the tight end angled quickly toward the middle of the field. Manny bolted over, but the pass was already there. He wrapped his arms tightly around the receiver and struggled to pull him down, slowing him enough that Donald could race over and finish the job. But the offense had made a first down.

Donald pulled Manny up. "Watch for that," he

said. "That's his favorite play. If I see it coming I'll give him a shot to slow him down. They'll run it again. Just watch."

A couple of running plays moved the ball ahead about 6 yards. It was third and four with the ball about 15 yards short of the end zone. Donald looked over and nodded.

The play began, and here came that tight end again. Donald slowed him slightly, but he was coming fast and looking at the quarterback. Manny shot in front of him as the ball came firing toward them. He got a hand on the ball and it deflected high, bonking off the tight end's shoulder pads and floating in the air. Manny leaped and grabbed it, coming down on one foot and pivoting quickly.

The tight end was off balance and Manny slipped away, trying to go wide and get out of the chaos. Two players got their hands on him, but he managed to pull free and raced toward the sideline, cutting upfield. Jason Fiorelli was all over him though and quickly brought him down.

Fiorelli grinned at Manny as he pinned him to

the ground. "Big-time interception," he said.

"We saw that play coming a mile away," Manny said.

"Yeah," Fiorelli said, shaking his head. "We're predictable, all right."

Coach Reynolds blew the whistle. "Nice job, defense," he said. "That's it for today. You eleven guys on defense line up at midfield. Everybody else take two laps and we'll see you back here tomorrow."

Manny and the others walked to midfield to wait for the coach.

"What's going on?" one of them asked.

"Special teams, I think," Donald said. "Probably the kickoff."

Donald was right. The coach set down his clipboard and rubbed his hands together in glee. "All right, gentlemen," he said. "There's a reason I had you out there together at the end of the scrimmage. To make you feel like a unit. You're about to participate in the most exciting play in football—the kickoff. You guys get to go full speed, full power, full throttle, and show the other team what we're made of. Let's do it!"

He lined up the eleven players across the field. Manny was the next-to-last man on the left side of the field, with Donald closest to the sideline.

"The end runs a box and in," Coach said to Donald. "Straight down the sideline and then straight across at about the twenty.

"You," he said, pointing to Manny, "go straight down, but angle in toward the ball carrier. If all goes right, this man next to you"—he pointed to Donald—"has the sideline cut off. The guy has nowhere to go but up the middle. He'll want to cut toward the sideline, so at least half the time it'll be you—or you"—he pointed to the guy one in from the other sideline—"who's got the first shot at making the tackle."

They ran through the motions a few times, with the coach hollering instructions to each player. "Monday we'll do it live, with a receiving team out there," he said. "Not bad for a first time tonight.

But we'll need a lot of work before next Saturday's game."

The game. Under the lights at home. If Hudson City kicked off to start the game, Manny would be on the field for the opening play.

All About Sports

Sal was up before six on the first day of school, eager to start kindergarten. Manny wanted to sleep, but he rolled out of bed at Sal's pleading and the brothers went downstairs. Dad was having coffee before leaving for work.

"I don't usually get company from you two so early," Dad said with a smile. "You must be excited about starting school."

Manny yawned. "I could do without it for a few more weeks," he said. "But this guy has been counting the seconds since midnight."

"I'm wearing my new sneakers," Sal said, climbing onto his father's lap. "And I already know how to read."

"I know," Dad said. "You'll be a lawyer or something before you know it."

"Or a football player," Sal said. "Like Manny."

"That reminds me," Manny said. "I'm hungry. What should we eat, Sal?"

"Cereal."

"Cereal. Yeah, I guess."

Mom came into the kitchen just then. "You're an early group," she said.

"We're working men," Sal said. "Today's the first day of school."

"I know," Mom said enthusiastically. "I'm going in to work late so I can drop you off, Sal."

"I thought Manny was going to walk me."

"He'll do that most days," Mom said. "Today is special. I'll probably cry when I drop you off."

"Not me," Sal said.

Mom gave Sal a kiss on the top of his head. "I know you won't," she said. "You'll be brave like Manny."

• • •

Manny fidgeted in his seat and looked at the clock. Just three minutes left in the first day of school. He couldn't wait to get out of there. Even the teacher was eager for the day to end—he'd halted class a few minutes early and told the kids to just look over their books and assignments.

Manny turned to big Anthony in the seat behind him. Anthony was looking through a magazine. He was nearly twice Manny's weight and fit tightly into a sixth-grade desk. The league weight limit was 155 pounds, and Anthony still had a few pounds to lose in order to be eligible.

"Anything good in there?" Manny asked.

"Some nice cars," Anthony said.

"Any sports articles?" Other kids his age were into music and clothing and cars, but for Manny it was all about sports.

"Not really." Anthony shrugged and closed the magazine. "You gain any weight?" he asked.

"I think I put on a pound or two," Manny said. "You lose any?"

Anthony gave an embarrassed smile. "About as much as you gained," he said. "I'm still three pounds over. I gotta starve myself the rest of the week."

Any suspect player had to be weighed in front of the opposing coaches right before every game. Anthony had been eight pounds too heavy when practice sessions started. Coach said he was bringing a scale to practice this afternoon. Anthony would be running a lot this week.

Anthony yawned and ran his hand over his short, bristly hair. "Practicing in that heat is wiping me out, Manny," he said. "I'm beat all the time."

"I don't have that problem," Manny said. "I'm spending too much time just watching you guys. I've got energy to spare."

"Yeah," Anthony said, shaking his head. "You don't play because you're too small, and I might not play because I'm too *big*."

The bell rang and Manny walked into the hallway and toward his locker. He could see Donald up ahead. They didn't have any classes together, but their lockers were next to each other on the second floor. Manny squeezed past a group of kids moving slowly and hurried to catch up to Donald.

"Slow down, young man," said a teacher.

Manny nodded and slowed down for about two steps. Then he caught Donald at the doorway to the stairs.

"One day down, a hundred eighty-one to go," Manny said.

"Can you believe I have homework in *three* subjects?" Donald said. "First day of school."

"Me, too," Manny said. "Well, in two of them we just have to put covers on the book."

"I'm wiped out," Donald said. "How do we get out of practice?"

"Why would you want to do that? Kickoff team, remember?"

"Oh, yeah."

They reached their lockers, but Manny's was occupied. Sherry Allegretta was leaning against it, chewing gum and looking at her watch.

"Excuse me," Manny said.

"You're excused." Sherry stared at him for a few seconds, then frowned and looked away.

"That's my locker."

"So?"

"I need to get in there."

Sherry sighed and rolled her eyes. She pushed away from the locker with her elbows and then leaned on the one next to it.

Manny worked his locker combination and tried not to lean into Sherry. She smelled strongly of gum and lip gloss. He could only open the locker about halfway because she was still taking up part of the space.

"Watch it," she said when Manny bumped her with the locker.

"You're in the way."

"I'm *waiting* for somebody."

"Well, can you wait, like, six inches farther over?"

Sherry sighed loudly again. "There he is anyway," she said as Jason Fiorelli walked down the hallway. Jason was a sports star with a great sense of humor and a mischievous smile. He was the one who'd tackled Manny after that interception the other day.

"Thanks a *lot*, squirt," Sherry said to Manny.

She was short but built. Manny watched her walk away, but Donald smacked his arm.

"We gotta go or we'll be late," Donald said. "She's out of your league, anyway."

"What? I ain't interested in *her*. She was just in my way," Manny said.

"Yeah, well, she's after Fiorelli," Donald said. "She can probably run him down faster than you could."

Manny laughed. "Yeah, but I hit harder."

"She'd better hit hard if she expects any time with Fiorelli," Donald said. "Every girl in the school seems to be after him."

CHAPTER 6

The Kickoff

*S*aturday came quickly, but the afternoon dragged on as Manny waited eagerly for game time. He watched a college game on TV and tossed a ball around with Sal, but every time he checked the clock it was only a little bit later than the time before.

Finally it was time to suit up, and he went to his closet to get his game jersey, where he'd hung it the day before. It felt smooth and new, with the white number 34 standing out from the bright red material. He'd even cleaned his helmet with window spray.

"You look like a pro," Sal said. "I can't wait for this game, Manny. I can't wait."

"I can't wait either. I hope we kick off. First play, I'm gonna nail somebody. *Wham!*"

"Knock 'em flat, Manny."

"Right on their butts."

Donald showed up a few minutes later, and they walked to the high school field. It was still two hours until game time, but the coaches wanted the players there by five P.M. to warm up and go over strategy. South Bergen had won the league title the year before, so the Hudson City Hornets were in for a battle.

"You nervous?" Donald asked as they arrived at the field.

"A little," Manny said. He laughed. "I think I'll be a *lot* more nervous when the game starts."

"Me, too. I hardly slept last night, and I could barely eat lunch."

"*You* not eating?" Manny said. "Never thought I'd see that."

"Oh, I ate. But I had to force it down."

Players were out on the field stretching and

throwing a football around. It wouldn't be dark for a while yet, but the lights would be on for the game.

Manny hadn't eaten much either, but his parents said they'd all go out for pizza after the game. He didn't even want to think about food, though. The jitters in his stomach told him he'd never keep anything down.

The team warmed up, did a few passing drills, and gathered around the head coach as he talked about playing smart and playing hard. "This is our home field, guys," he said. "Don't let them take over our turf. Show them who's boss, right from the opening play."

The team yelled. Game time was approaching quickly. The bleachers were filled with spectators, and the referees had arrived, gathering near midfield in their black-and-white uniforms. The South Bergen team, dressed in white uniforms with blue-and-yellow trim, looked big and strong on the opposite sideline.

Manny looked around for Anthony and saw him

trotting onto the field from the locker room. Anthony made a fist and shook it in the air as he saw Manny. "One pound under!" he shouted.

"Yeah!" Manny yelled. Anthony had made it under the weight limit.

"All I ate since lunch yesterday was two crackers with peanut butter," Anthony said as he reached the sideline.

Wide receiver Jason Fiorelli came over and put his arms around Anthony, pretending that he was going to pick him up. "You're light as a feather," Jason said, joking as always.

Manny was amazed that Fiorelli never seemed to give in to pressure. He'd seen him go to the line in the final seconds of the YMCA championship basketball game and calmly sink two free throws to secure a victory. One time he made three straight strikes in the tenth frame of a bowling match when anything less would have meant a loss. And he always did these things with a smile on his face. Here they were, seconds from the kickoff, and Jason was as loose as ever.

"Listen, Anthony, if you're hungry, you can

graze between plays," Fiorelli said. "Just take a mouthful of grass."

"I'm ready to eat my helmet," Anthony said.

"Think of their quarterback as a big hunk of steak," Fiorelli said. "Every time you sack him, you get to take a bite."

"Maybe I'll picture a turkey instead," Anthony said. "Steaks don't run away from you."

Vinnie DiMarco and the other captain walked to the center of the field for the coin flip. Manny swallowed hard. South Bergen won the toss and the official indicated that they'd be receiving.

"Kickoff team, get ready!" yelled an assistant coach.

Manny snapped his chinstrap and closed his eyes. First play of the season, and he'd be out there. Anthony smacked him on the helmet and said, "Let's go, Manny. Use that speed."

The crowd stood and cheered as the Hornets took the field. Manny and Donald jogged to their spots near the opposite sideline. South Bergen players were glaring at them from across the field. The guy across from Manny was huge.

"Box and in," Manny said to Donald.

"I know it," Donald said. "Get ready to sprint your butt off, man. Straight down and angle in. Stop that sucker cold."

DiMarco was lined up to kick, raising his hand to signal for his teammates to move. The crowd continued to yell. Manny took one last gulp of air and rubbed his hands together.

There! The kick was high and long, slicing toward Manny's side of the field. Manny streaked ahead, watching the receiver as he waited for the ball.

Suddenly Manny felt a major impact as his legs were cut from underneath and he went sprawling toward the grass. He hit the ground hard, but scrambled up and searched for the return man.

There he was, cutting straight toward him. Manny took a quick step in that direction, but another blocker was leading the way. Manny was no match for him, getting knocked aside and spinning to the turf once again. The ball carrier ran past, crossing midfield, racing along the sideline.

DiMarco finally made the tackle down near the

20-yard line. He'd saved a touchdown, but South Bergen had great field position for its opening series.

Manny got up and jogged across the field. Donald was just ahead of him, hobbling a bit.

Donald turned to Manny. "What happened?" he asked.

"I got wiped out after about two seconds," Manny said. "Knocked on my butt. Twice."

"Me, too. That was terrible."

"Those dudes are big," Manny said. "And fast."

"So are we," Donald said. "They just got lucky."

They reached the sideline and the assistant coach called them over.

"Guys, that wasn't pretty," the coach said. "We had no penetration. We gave them a clear path up the field. You guys on the end"—he pointed to Donald and Manny—"you have to close off those lanes. Stay on your feet and hit back."

They both nodded vigorously. Manny wasn't sure what he could have done differently though. He never had a chance to get downfield.

South Bergen's great field position was too

much for the Hudson City defense to overcome. The opponents had a rugged fullback who bulled through the line repeatedly. A quick pass into the end zone capped the drive, and South Bergen was ahead.

Hudson City didn't get far on its first opportunity, being left 4 yards short of a first down on its opening series. DiMarco's punt left South Bergen well short of midfield, however, and the Hornets' defense was able to hold them this time.

The first half became little more than a succession of punts, as neither team made a serious drive downfield. It was still 7–0 at halftime.

"We're right in this one," Coach Reynolds told his players in the locker room. "Our defense has been great, and the offense is starting to show something. We need to get a score and even this one up. This second half should belong to us."

Donald smacked Manny on the arm. "After we score, you and me are gonna make up for that screw-up on the kickoff," he said. "This time we nail 'em deep in their territory. Maybe even cause a fumble on the return."

Manny swallowed hard and nodded. "You said it."

Hudson City received the second-half kickoff and established good field position. Then, facing third and five, DiMarco dropped back to pass. His speedy wide receiver, Jason Fiorelli, had raced past the defender and was open downfield. DiMarco let loose with a long spiraling pass, and the crowd stood in anticipation. But the ball fell short. Fiorelli reached back to grab it, but the defender was there first, hauling it in for an interception and stopping Hudson City's drive.

Manny shook his head hard. "Man, that was a sure touchdown."

"Not enough of an arm," Donald said. "That was just too far."

The game remained a defensive struggle, with neither team able to get past midfield. Finally, midway through the fourth quarter, DiMarco found Fiorelli on a shorter pass across the middle. Fiorelli streaked downfield, getting a crucial block from another of the ends, and ran untouched into the end zone. DiMarco's kick tied the score at 7–7, and the Hudson City players and fans went wild.

"All right!" Manny shouted. "Let's hold 'em now. Hold 'em on defense and get that ball back."

Donald grabbed his arm. "Forget the yelling. It's up to us."

"What is?"

"The kickoff. Duh. We scored. Let's get out there."

Manny had been so excited by the touchdown that he'd forgotten what came next. He sprinted onto the field, determined to make up for that opening kickoff.

"Let's go!" Donald shouted.

"In their faces!" Manny shouted back. He looked up at the scoreboard. Nearly four minutes still remained; plenty of time for Hudson City to get that ball back and win the game.

"Penetrate!" came the call from the sideline. Manny glared down the field and exhaled furiously.

There was the kick, straight and high. The receiver was under it at about the 15-yard line. Manny and Donald sprinted up the field.

That same blocker was ahead of him, but Manny was thinking this time. He gave a quick feint toward the sideline, then burst past the blocker, angling toward the middle of the field. The ball carrier was headed his way, and Manny had a clear shot. His eyes opened wide and he darted toward the runner, intent on stopping him cold. Two more steps and he'd have him.

The *crack* of shoulder pad against shoulder pad sent Manny sailing, spinning to the ground as the runner brushed past him. Manny had been blind-sided by another blocker just as he was about to make the tackle.

Not again! Manny thought as he rolled to his feet, sprinting behind the return man who was now 20 yards ahead of him with a clear field ahead. Even DiMarco couldn't catch him this time, and the runner reached the end zone and held the ball above his head. His teammates raced over and surrounded him, jumping up and down and yelling.

Manny stood there stunned, his mouth hanging open in disbelief. A South Bergen player, jogging onto the field for the extra point, gave Manny a shove. "Get off the field."

"Screw you," Manny said, but he turned and ran off.

The coaches were shaking their heads and frowning. "You guys are killing us," Coach Reynolds said in the direction of the kickoff-team players who were scrunched together near the bench.

Manny took a seat and left his helmet on, staring at the ground. Two kickoffs, two letdowns. Both times the ball carrier had run right through Manny's territory.

"Let's get it back," the coach shouted toward the field. He clapped his hands. "Plenty of time left. Let's go!"

There *was* plenty of time, but Hudson City couldn't do much with it. Two passes fell incomplete, and a third went for little yardage. On fourth down, DiMarco threw another long, wobbly pass that was knocked down by the cornerback. South Bergen ran out the clock, and Hudson City lost, 14–7.

"We're dead," Donald said to Manny. "That was all our fault."

"I know," Manny said. "We blew it."

Coach Reynolds gathered the team around him. "All right, guys, we have some work to do," he said. "Our defense was outstanding. The offense needs a bit of fine-tuning, but we'll be okay. Special teams . . . well, we may have to make a few changes there. But that was a very good football team we lost to tonight. We gave them a tough battle. Have a great weekend, and we'll get back to work on Monday."

Benched?

Manny looked at his half-eaten slice of pizza and set it on the plate. The bite in his mouth was as thick as paste. He swallowed hard and shook his head, looking around the restaurant.

"Cheer up, Manny," Donald said. "We'll practice hard all week and be better next time."

Manny let out a heavy exhale. "Didn't you hear what he said? Changes on the special teams. Who would *you* change if you were the coach? You'd start with the guy who got run over on both kickoffs."

Manny's dad patted him on the shoulder. "Maybe not," he said. "Maybe he just meant a different approach, a different strategy."

"Yeah," Donald said. "He never said he'd use different players."

Manny rolled his eyes. "Forget it," he said. "I'm benched. I screwed up."

"They'd never bench you, Manny," Sal said. "You're the best player on the team!"

Manny gave a half-hearted laugh. "Thanks, Sal."

"You'll feel better if you eat," said Mom. "You've hardly eaten anything all day."

Manny loved the pizza at the Grotto, but tonight it tasted like cardboard. He knew he'd failed miserably in his first football game. He knew he'd cost his team the game.

"I'm not hungry, Mom," he said. "Maybe we can take some of this home and I'll eat it later."

"You're feeling all right, though?" she asked. "I hate to see you looking so down."

"I feel fine, Mom. I'm just mad. I'm not five years old, you know. I won't fall apart from being angry."

They sat in silence for a few moments, chewing their pizza. Finally Sal spoke up.

"I'm five, Manny," he said. "And I won't fall apart. I'll be just as mad as you are, okay? We'll both stay mad until the next game. Then you'll make that tackle."

Manny reached across the table. He shook his brother's hand and said, "Okay, Sal, it's a deal. We'll both stay just a little bit mad all week. And if the coach gives me another chance, I'll be sure not to screw it up."

If the coach gave him another chance. Manny knew that was no sure thing.

Manny's appetite was back by Sunday morning, and he ate a huge breakfast before church. But all during the sermon he thought about those kickoffs, how he'd been so overpowered by the blockers.

He was quiet in the car during the ride home.

"The Giants are on at one," Dad said. "Playing the Cowboys. Should be a good one."

"Yeah," Manny said. "I'm gonna go for a run first. Over to the track."

"Don't you need a rest?" Dad asked. "You're not tired from the game?"

Manny rolled his eyes. "I was only in for two plays," he said. "And I spent most of the time on the ground."

Manny needed to burn off some energy, but he also needed to think. Running would be a good way to do that. He changed into a gray Yankees tank top and a pair of soccer shorts and jogged to the high school field, right where he'd played the night before. The stadium was empty now, but the gate was open.

Manny was warm already, so he began running quickly around the hard-rubber track. As he reached the back straightaway, he fell into thinking about those kickoffs again. He took a sidestep to avoid an imaginary blocker, then dodged ahead in a sprint. Here came another blocker, and Manny lowered his shoulder to take the blow, then pushed off and continued on his way.

He reached the turn and ran a little slower, taking a deep breath of the warm, moist air. Then he got to the front stretch and started moving fast again, seeing those blockers coming toward him, scrambling out of their way. This was fun. He imagined that the crowd was cheering as he blasted toward the ball carrier, whacking him hard and knocking the ball from his grasp. He scooped up the loose ball and raced toward the end zone, flying in untouched for a score.

Manny ran eight laps like that, two full miles, jogging on the turns and sprinting on the straightaways. He was sweating heavily and panting hard, but he felt good now. He'd be ready next time. He wouldn't go down so easily.

He wasn't big, but he was quick. He'd have to avoid getting hit by the bigger blockers, or dodge enough to minimize the impact. Playing smart was just as important as playing tough. He could take the hits, but maybe next time he'd get the chance to dish one out instead.

Never Quit

"At least we're keeping our uniforms clean," Donald said to Manny as they kneeled on the sideline at Monday's practice. Except for some warm-up laps and calisthenics, the subs hadn't had much to do.

Coach Reynolds had kept his starters in for the entire scrimmage, hoping to build more consistency in the offense. He hadn't said much about the loss to South Bergen, just that he hoped his team had learned a few things in the game and that there was still a long season ahead.

"We might even meet them again in the playoffs," Coach said. "I think we've got the best defense in the league. If we can establish a running game over the next few weeks, then we'll be a tough team to beat."

Nothing had been mentioned about the special teams, but maybe that would come later in the week.

"Think we're still on the kickoff team?" Manny asked Donald.

Donald just shrugged. "Don't know. I started worrying about it Saturday night though. A lot. I threw up that pizza when I got home."

"I probably would have, too, if I'd eaten any," Manny said. "I felt better yesterday after I ran. I just needed to do something, you know? There was nobody to hit, so I just ran my butt off."

"I watched TV all afternoon," Donald said. "That didn't help much."

"Giants won."

"I saw it."

Manny kicked at the dirt. "Think we'll get in today?"

"Doesn't look like it."

They stayed put for fifteen more minutes until the coach blew his whistle, then ran three laps with the rest of the team. Manny finished well ahead of everyone else again, having plenty of unused energy.

"I'm supposed to be gaining weight," Manny said after the run, walking off the field with Anthony. "If all I do is run, I'll never put on any pounds."

"Maybe you could run behind me and pick up all the weight I'm shedding," Anthony said with a grin. "I'm down five pounds since last Monday." Anthony patted his belly. "But I'm constantly hungry."

"Me, too," Manny said. "You've just got a bigger place to hold the food."

"Yeah, but it's getting smaller," Anthony said. "See you tomorrow at school."

Donald and Manny walked toward home, carrying their cleats in their helmets. The air was less humid as autumn approached, but the days were still quite warm.

"We getting something to eat?" Donald asked.

"Yeah. But I'm not going in there if you're going to rip them off again."

"I won't," Donald said. "I told my dad about that apple pie and he made me go back and pay for it."

"Really? Why didn't you tell me?"

"I didn't think it was any big deal."

"What did they say at the store when you went back?" Manny asked.

"Not much," Donald said. "I didn't exactly tell them what happened. I just handed the guy at the cash register a dollar and said they'd under-charged me for something. He goes 'Well, it's great to meet an honest young man.' I just smiled and walked out. Mr. Honesty."

Manny laughed. "I almost went back and paid them *for* you. I figured I was just as guilty for let-ting you do it."

They'd reached the grocery store. Manny reached into his sock and took out a dollar bill. "My mom's making rice and beans for dinner. I can pig out on that. All I need right now is a soda."

"Me, too," Donald said. "I wanna get home. I've got a ton of homework."

"Think we'll spend the rest of the season sitting on our butts?" Manny asked.

"I don't know. Coach Reynolds is a good guy. I think he *wants* to let everybody play. We just have to take advantage when we do. We've got another tough game this week, and he wants to make sure the starters are ready for it."

"Well, if we're going to be benchwarmers, at least we're getting good practice for that," Manny said with a laugh.

They walked down the aisle and Manny picked up a box of Frosted Flakes. "Sal loves this stuff," he said.

"Me, too," Donald said. "I eat it by the handful right out of the box."

They walked around the store, looking at the piles of apples and pears and stopping to stare at the big bags of pretzels and potato chips. When they'd made it back to the cash registers, they each got a bottle of soda and continued on their way.

Across the street, in the field behind St. Joseph's Church, Manny could see his old soccer team practicing. "Let's go over there for a minute," he said.

They crossed the Boulevard and walked onto the field, stopping next to the young priest who coached the squad.

"Hey, Father Lou," Manny said.

"Hey, guys," the priest said. "How's it going?"

"Not bad."

"We could use you, Manny. Not enough speed in the midfield this year."

Manny nodded. "I may be back next season. You never know."

They watched the players on the field, moving the ball quickly back and forth. The parish team was always good, but Manny could tell they were a bit less skilled than usual.

"How's football going?" Father Lou asked.

"It's fun," Manny said. "But we don't play that much."

"We're specialists," Donald said.

Father Lou smiled. "That's important, too."

A fifth grader came racing down the field, dribbling the ball with skill and feinting past two defenders. He made a nice centering pass to a teammate, who booted the ball into the goal. Father Lou clapped his hands and said, "Nice one, fellas. That's the way."

Donald grabbed Manny's sleeve and gave a tug. "We gotta get going," he said.

"Yeah," Manny said, still staring at the field. "See ya, Father."

"Thanks for stopping by, boys."

"Okay."

Manny looked back as they reached the fence. The soccer players had started scrimmaging again.

"I'd be a starter on that team," Manny said.

Donald shrugged. "You could probably still get on the team . . . if you wanted to."

Manny stood still for a moment. He looked over at Father Lou. "Nah," he finally said. "I don't quit at anything. And I like football. Even if I hardly ever play."

They walked toward home, a little more slowly than usual.

"I figured we'd make our mark on the kickoff team, then get more and more playing time on defense," Manny said. "Looks like the opposite is happening. We messed up our chances on the kickoff team, and now we'll be doing nothing the rest of the season."

"Maybe, maybe not," Donald said. "Look, give it another week. If we don't start playing again, at least in practice, then we'll *ask* for another shot. Besides, we don't even know yet if we're off the kickoff team or not. He still didn't say that we were."

"Yeah. You're right," Manny said. "But it sure didn't look good for us today."

Bad News

Sal was waiting, as usual, on the front steps of the house as Manny walked up the block. When he saw his big brother coming, he ran up the sidewalk to meet him.

"Hi, Sal, how's it going?" Manny said, bending down to give his brother a hug.

"I was worried," Sal said.

"About what?"

"About football practice," Sal said. "I didn't want you to get in trouble."

Manny put his hand on Sal's shoulder as they began to walk. "No trouble," Manny said. "I didn't get to do much today, but nobody yelled at me."

"That's good."

"Yeah. Here, you can carry my helmet."

"Are we still mad, Manny?"

Manny laughed. "I don't think so, buddy. Determined, but not mad. We'll get another chance . . . I think."

"You'll clobber 'em, Manny."

"You said it, Sal."

"Did you make any great plays today?" Sal asked.

"No. I didn't do much of anything. Coach was working with the starters all day. We've got another tough game this week."

They entered the kitchen and Manny gave his mom a hug.

"Hi, sweetie," she said. "We're running late. I had a meeting and your dad's swamped with work, so dinner won't be for a while."

"That's okay," Manny said. "Me and Sal will set the table and do whatever else you need. I'll get cleaned up first."

"That's great."

After he showered, Manny sat on the bedroom floor with Sal and helped him build a tower with Legos.

"How come we're not big, Manny?" Sal asked.

"I don't know. We just aren't. Dad's small. Mom's small. So we are, too."

"I'm gonna be giant," Sal said. "I'm gonna be a quarterback."

Manny laughed. "Don't count on it. Dad weighs less than some of the guys on my team, and they're only in sixth grade."

"I'll lift weights."

"That's good. But small guys can do a lot of things, Sal. We're usually faster, too."

"Yeah . . . I guess I don't want to be big, Manny. I wanna be just like you."

"Thanks, buddy. Now let's go set the table for dinner."

The bad news came at Wednesday's practice, when Coach Reynolds called the kickoff team together.

"We got burned twice last Saturday, fellas, and

that really hurt our chances to win the game. This week we play over in Newark, and that's another very powerful team. You know that I want every player on this team to get a fair shot, but we need to make some changes on the kickoff squad. Our left side is a little weak, so for now I'm putting a few of the defensive starters there. We'll re-evaluate things as the season goes on."

Manny, Donald, and two others were off the kickoff team for now, replaced by the starting line-backers and Jason Fiorelli. The displaced players headed off the field to watch the kickoff squad go through the drill.

Manny kneeled at the sideline but kept his helmet on, blinking back a few tears. Donald paced back and forth, muttering to himself and smacking his fist in his hand. The other players stood silently, watching the action on the field.

Finally Donald came over and kneeled next to Manny. "This sucks," he said. "All we needed was some experience. We got that last week. We'd have no problem this week, I guarantee it. We'd stop those suckers cold."

Manny just stared at the field. Eventually Anthony came over and stood next to him. Anthony was way too slow for the kickoff team, but he was the anchor of the offensive and defensive lines. So he was in for every play except the kicks. Manny's eyes only came up to the level of Anthony's shoulder pads.

"How you doin', Manny?" Anthony asked.

Manny shrugged.

"We could use your speed on those kickoffs," Anthony said. "But I guess what we mostly needed was a little more strength."

"Yeah," Manny said softly. "I got pushed all over the field last week."

"Well, don't feel too bad. Those guys were big. Even *I* got pushed around a little. 'Course, I pushed back pretty good."

Donald stepped closer, punching Anthony lightly on the arm. "We just weren't thinking," Donald said. "I mean, that was our first game. Give us another week of practice and we'd be unbeatable."

"Well, Coach said he'd re-evaluate," Anthony

said. "I hope so. You guys deserve to be playing. Maybe this isn't the end."

"It better not be," Manny said. He sniffed hard and spit. "We've been working too hard to spend the rest of the season on the sideline."

Left Out

The game in Newark was on Sunday afternoon, so Manny's family went to the early mass. The bus was to leave at eleven, so Manny hustled to get his uniform on, and his dad drove him to the school.

"See you at the game," Dad said.

"Right," Manny said. He was looking forward to the game, but this was nothing like the week before, when he'd had a hollow, nervous feeling, knowing he'd be in the spotlight on those kickoffs. Today he'd be little more than a spectator. He missed the anxiety of the week before.

Donald and Manny sat together on the bus. Players whooped and smacked each other, getting psyched up for the game, but the two of them stayed pretty quiet. Manny didn't even feel like part of the team.

Coach Reynolds gathered the players at the sideline just before the kickoff. "This is one tough league we play in, gentlemen. Week after week, we go against big, quick opponents. We lost a tight one last week, but a win here today will get us right back in the race. Are we ready?"

"Yes!" shouted the players.

"I said, *Are we ready?*"

"Yes!" they yelled even louder.

Coach was quiet for a few seconds. "Then let's do it," he said.

"Let's go!"

The players spread out along the sideline, waiting for the kickoff. Hudson City was receiving the ball. Manny bounced up and down a few times, feeling a surge of energy. The day was the coolest in quite a while, just right for a football game. Manny was ready to hit somebody, to bring somebody down. But it didn't seem likely that would happen.

Hudson City mounted a short drive on its first possession, but wound up punting before reaching midfield. The Newark team didn't have much luck either, and Fiorelli broke a long return on the Newark punt, sprinting down the sideline in front of the Hudson City bench as his teammates shouted and leaped.

Fiorelli stumbled slightly as he crossed the 10-yard line, enabling a Newark player to tackle him from behind. But the Hornets had a first-and-goal opportunity.

"Let's punch it in!" Coach Reynolds yelled as the offense took the field.

Vinnie DiMarco called signals and took the snap. He handed the ball to the fullback, Jared Owen, who barreled ahead nearly to the goal line before being stopped. DiMarco dove into the end zone on a quarterback sneak on the very next play, and his extra-point kick gave Hudson City a 7–0 lead.

"That's the way!" Coach called. "Kickoff team on the field!"

Manny felt a sudden chill as the coach called for the kickoff unit. *That should be me*, he thought. He glanced over at Donald, who was looking out at the field with a scowl.

Manny turned toward the bleachers. He knew right where his parents and Sal were sitting. He hadn't told them he was no longer on the kickoff squad. Sal was standing, looking up and down the field. Manny turned back to the game. He swallowed hard.

The kickoff team did its job, and Newark began at its own 25. The home team had a pair of strong running backs, and they began to find their groove. Eating up 4 or 5 yards at a time, Newark moved down the field, using an occasional short pass to keep the defense on their toes. The drive ate up several minutes and was capped by a 7-yard end-around dash into the end zone.

Newark attempted to take the lead with a two-point conversion, counting on their fullback to hammer it in for the score. But Anthony muscled past his blocker and filled the hole quickly, bringing the ball carrier down short of the goal line. So Hudson City retained the lead, 7–6.

Halftime came, and Coach Reynolds was pleased. "They haven't broken any big gains on us," he said. "If we can contain those running backs in the second half, we should come out of here with a win."

Manny jogged back to the field with his teammates. He wasn't likely to get any playing time in a game as close as this one, but he'd be ready if the chance arrived.

"Great play on that extra-point attempt," he said to Anthony.

"I was mad that they'd been running all over us on that drive," Anthony said. "Had to do something big."

"You did it."

Fiorelli stuck his head between them. "The goalposts were rattling after that tackle," he said. "Anthony made the ground shake."

"We are lightning and thunder, Jason," Anthony said. "You got the speed and I got the power."

Manny took a good look at his two teammates. They had everything he didn't have—strength, height, confidence. Fiorelli jogged onto the field. Anthony rested a hand on Manny's shoulder. "Hope you get to play some," he said.

"So do I."

Hudson City kicked off to start the second half, and again stopped Newark well upfield. Manny had to admit that the new lineup was working.

Late in the third quarter, Hudson City had the ball near midfield, facing a third down and seven. Everyone in the stadium expected a pass play.

"Got to get it to Jason," Manny whispered to Donald.

Jason Fiorelli was split wide. Manny and everyone else had expected DiMarco to be the star of this team, but it seemed as if Jason was emerging as the standout.

DiMarco dropped back and looked toward the secondary, searching for an open receiver. Seeing no one, he rolled toward the sideline, tucking the ball close to his chest and trying to run for it. But just before crossing the line of scrimmage, he spotted Fiorelli angling back toward the sideline, a step or two ahead of the defender.

DiMarco stopped in his tracks and heaved the ball toward Fiorelli, who stretched to his maximum and caught the pass with his fingertips. He hauled it in close and never broke stride, running straight to the end zone for the touchdown.

Fiorelli jogged over to the bench and slapped hands with his teammates. Donald smacked him on the shoulder. DiMarco's kick made it 14–6, and the Hornets and their fans could sense a victory on the way.

The defense remained steady, forcing Newark to punt on its next possession. Anthony stopped the next opportunity with a ferocious sack of the quarterback on a fourth-down play in Hudson City territory.

DiMarco then led a steady, time-consuming drive for Hudson City as the fourth quarter wound down, finally connecting with Fiorelli on another touchdown pass that all but sealed the victory.

Coach Reynolds made a fist and pumped his

arm. He grabbed hold of Fiorelli and shook his hand. "Take a rest," he said. "You've earned it."

Coach looked around. "Donald!" he shouted. "Get out there for the kickoff. Give Jason the break he's earned. Let's do it!"

Donald jammed his helmet onto his head and quickly snapped the chinstrap as he ran onto the field. Manny stood alone on the sideline.

The kick was high and deep, giving the Hornets a good chance to get downfield before the runback. The return man fielded the ball and hesitated slightly, not sure which way up the field would be best. He cut toward the sideline and angled upfield, but Donald and two others were right in his path. The runner gave a juke and turned back to the center of the field, then eluded one tackler and swerved back toward the sideline. Donald hit him low and another hit him high, and the kickoff team had its third straight stop without any major runbacks.

Donald came racing off the field with his fist in the air. He jumped the last two yards to the sideline, landing with both feet right next to Manny.

"*Big-time* hit!" Donald said. "Squashed that guy like a bug."

"Nice job," Manny said, trying as hard as he could to sound enthusiastic.

Donald walked over to the bench, joining the other kickoff team members, who were laughing and pounding each other. "We're back in business!" Donald said.

Manny let out his breath and looked at the field. That could have been him.

But it wasn't.

The Wrong
Sport?

Manny sat quietly on the bus ride back to Hudson City, looking out the window as his teammates celebrated the victory. Donald was next to him, but he kneeled on his seat and faced the back of the bus, shouting and laughing like the others.

"Come on, Manny," Donald finally said. "We kicked their butts! Get into it."

Manny forced a smile, but he didn't feel like cheering. He slumped in his seat a bit more and waited for the bus ride to end.

"We're all going over to McDonald's to

celebrate," Donald said as they got off the bus. "You coming?"

"I don't think so," Manny said. "Not hungry."

"So what?" Donald said. "Get a soda."

"Nah," Manny said. "My parents wanted me to get right home after the game."

"How come?"

"I don't know." Actually, Manny's parents had said that they *didn't* expect him home right away. But he didn't feel like being with the team. He didn't even feel like *part* of the team.

So Manny walked home alone. His parents and Sal were watching TV.

"Hi, Manny!" Sal said. "You guys won!"

"Yeah," Manny said glumly. "No thanks to me."

"Well, you'll get 'em next time," Dad said. "Keep your chin up."

"I know."

"You would've scored three touchdowns if they'd let you play!" Sal said.

Manny frowned. "Don't kid yourself, Sal," he said. "I wouldn't score a touchdown if I played for six years."

Sal just stared at his brother with his mouth open. Manny never spoke to him like that.

"Get over it, squirt," Manny said sharply. "Don't hold your breath waiting for me to be a hero."

Sal looked stunned, then he blinked back tears. Manny felt awful for hurting Sal's feelings, but the little guy would have to deal with it. It was hard enough for Manny to know that he was no football star without Sal pretending all the time that he was.

Manny turned with a sigh and plodded up the stairs. He shut the bedroom door and took off his uniform and pads. There wasn't a speck of dirt on them, of course. He changed into shorts and a T-shirt and walked back down the stairs. It wouldn't be dark yet for more than an hour.

"I'm going for a walk," he told his parents.

"Where to?" said Mom.

"Just around. A run, actually. I've got a lot of energy to burn."

"You weren't nice to Sal," Mom said.

"I know, Mom. He'll live."

Manny ran along a side street, then cut over to Central Avenue, running parallel to the Boulevard.

As he neared St. Joseph's Church, he heard shouting. His old soccer team was having a game.

The scoreboard said Home 2, Visitor 1, and showed about three minutes left in the game. Manny watched from outside the fence as his team held off a frantic offensive charge by their opponents and hung on for a narrow win.

He missed that feeling of running down the field, his legs and the ball moving almost as one. The jittery little fakes and jukes as he worked his way through the defense, finding an open teammate or taking it to the goal by himself.

Maybe next year. Or maybe the coach had been right when he'd suggested cross-country. Manny could run all day. Football wasn't looking like the right sport for him these days.

He took off again, running a bit faster now, excited by the soccer game. He headed to the track and ran a few laps, then walked the half mile back to his house.

"Worked up a sweat, I see," Dad said as Manny entered the living room.

"Yeah." Manny gave a small smile. "Couldn't do

it at the football game; had to find my own way."

"That's what it's about," Dad said. "You always have to find your own way."

Manny shut the door to his room and sat on the bed, turning on the radio to a New York City rock station. Sal was downstairs with their parents, so Manny had more time to think.

After a while, he heard his mom calling from downstairs. He opened the door and said, "What?"

"You've got a visitor."

"Send him up." Manny sat back on his bed. He figured it was Donald, ready to gloat a little more about that tackle he'd made. He'd listen, but he was still in no mood for celebrating. Manny was glad for Donald, but he wasn't quite over his jealousy.

But then there was a knock on the doorframe, and Anthony peered into the room. He was wearing his game jersey. Even without the pads, the jersey was stretched tight across his big body.

"Hey!" Manny said, getting to his feet in a hurry. "What are you doing here?"

Anthony shrugged and grinned. "I don't know.

You weren't at McDonald's with the team. Figured I should check up on you."

"I wasn't hungry."

"I sure was." Anthony laughed. "It killed me to see what everybody else was eating, though. First time I been there in months." He grabbed his belly, which was smaller but still hefty. "Diet soda and no fries. I might as well live on lettuce."

Manny laughed, too, but then he turned away. "I just didn't feel like being there."

"Why not?"

"Hardly felt like part of the team."

"Ah, that's crazy," Anthony said. He wiped the corner of his mouth with a finger and looked at it. "Ketchup." He grinned. "Manny, you put the pads on every day just like the rest of us. You work your butt off when you get the chance. You're just as much a part of the team as I am."

"Thanks. I don't buy it, but that's nice of you to say it."

"Everybody was asking where you were tonight," Anthony said. "I mean it. We all like you, Manny."

At that moment Sal burst into the room and grabbed Anthony by the leg. "He sacks the big guy!" Sal yelled.

Anthony put his hands on Sal's shoulders and rolled gently to the floor. "Oh, man!" Anthony said. "This guy is a monster!"

Anthony tickled Sal until he let go. Sal leaped to his feet. "You're huge!" he said.

"I like food," Anthony said. "My mom's a heck of a cook."

"So is my mom," Sal said. "But I'm puny."

"That don't matter," Anthony said. "You'll grow. Now, what can we do to cheer up your brother here? What kind of game can we play?"

"Chutes and Ladders?" Sal asked. "That's my favorite game."

"Mine, too," said Anthony, winking at Manny. "Set it up. I'll kick your butt. Manny's, too."

"Yeah, set it up," said Manny, patting Sal's shoulder. "Let's get this game under way. Let's get things back to normal."

Something Different

*M*anny stuck with football, of course, spending most of the practice time watching the others. After calisthenics and a series of drills each afternoon, the better players would scrimmage while a small group of subs gathered on the sideline, watching and waiting.

Another game came and went, with the Hornets squeaking out a 14–13 win at home. For the second straight game, Manny stayed on the sideline.

By Wednesday of the following week, the coaching staff seemed satisfied that the team was ready for another good performance. They'd be playing at Palisades, a few miles up the road, on Sunday afternoon. Palisades was 0–3, but Coach Reynolds made it clear during practice that this wouldn't be an easy game.

Late in the day, one of the assistant coaches walked over to the sideline. "We're almost done," he said to the group that was kneeling there. "Let's get you guys in for a few plays." He counted them quickly. "Six of you."

The coach set his hand on Donald's shoulder. "Fullback." He pointed to Manny. "Wing." He sent another player in at tailback and told the three others to take spots on the defense.

"We're playing offense?" Manny said.

"Yeah, why not?" the coach said. "No harm in trying something different."

Coach Reynolds was calling the plays in the huddle, but DiMarco was still in at quarterback. "Hmmm, the mini-backfield," Coach said. "Okay. We'll keep it basic. Tailback off right tackle. Fullback, you lead the way. On three."

"What do I do?" Manny asked.

"Block the middle linebacker. Let's go."

Manny lined up behind the tight end, listening to the signals. He'd never played offense before.

The ball was snapped and Manny shot into the defensive backfield, zeroing in on the linebacker. He lowered his shoulder into the defender's ribs, churning with his feet as the running back slipped behind him. A 3-yard gain. Not bad.

"Your turn, Donald," Coach said in the huddle. "We'll go with a quick count, on one. Inside left tackle this time."

Donald scooted ahead for about 4 yards, but the ball popped loose as a cornerback came up and hit him hard. Manny dove toward the ball, but big Anthony was on it, saving the ball for the offense.

"Crud," Donald said as he peeled himself off the ground. He looked at his hands. "How could I lose that?"

"Gotta cover that ball up when you're in the trenches," Coach said. "Anthony saved you. We need two yards for a first down." He looked around the huddle. "Let's have some fun. Wingback." He touched Manny's shoulder. Manny felt a chill right down to his stomach. "At the snap, you come straight toward DiMarco for the pitch," Coach said. "You follow him right over Anthony. They'll move all those bodies out of the way for you. Let's do it."

Manny trotted over to his spot behind the end and stared straight ahead. He knew from playing defense that the linebackers would be watching the running backs' eyes, hoping for a clue as to which way the play was going.

DiMarco called signals, then took the snap. Manny pivoted toward the backfield and saw the ball floating toward him. He grabbed it and followed the quarterback through the hole. Anthony had driven his opponent out of the way, and DiMarco was taking down the middle linebacker. Manny darted through the opening and saw a clear field ahead, but the hole was quickly filled by the safety.

Manny dodged left, then shifted back to the right, gripping the ball tightly to his chest with both arms. He was 5 yards past the line of scrimmage, now 10, and two defensive players were on him, bringing him down.

"Nice gain!" Coach shouted. "Great blocking up front."

Manny set down the ball and pumped his fist. He jogged back to the huddle, and DiMarco smacked him on the shoulder. "Good job," he said.

"All right, way to move the ball, Manny," Coach said. "We've got time for a few more plays. Let's see if we can get it into the end zone."

He called another run for Donald. "Hold it tight," he said.

This time Donald held on, but he managed to gain only a yard. The tailback carried twice for a few more yards, but they were still 30 yards from the end zone.

"Okay," Coach said. "Final play, then we run a few laps and head for home. We'll run a quarter-back option, but we're looking for a pass. Manny, I want you to do a ten-yard square out and watch for the ball."

Manny nodded. At the snap he ran straight upfield, gave a little juke, and cut straight toward the sideline. He was wide open, but where was DiMarco? He could see a wave of defenders in the backfield, and suddenly Coach was blowing the whistle. DiMarco had been sacked.

Could have been a touchdown, Manny thought. *Oh well, that was fun anyway.*

Manny hadn't had many chances, but he'd done some good things this season, at least in practice. There was the time he chased down DiMarco and stopped a touchdown, the pass interception, a terrific run with the ball this afternoon.

He was starting to feel like a football player again.

Another Chance

*G*ame day. Sal sat on his bed with Manny's helmet on his lap and watched his brother get into his pads and uniform.

"Do you think you'll play today, Manny?" Sal asked.

"Maybe, Sal. You never know. This is a game we should win, so guys like me and Donald might get some playing time."

"I hope so, Manny."

"I hope so, too."

Sal put the helmet on his own head. It covered his eyes.

"Not quite," Manny said with a laugh. "Your head's not fat enough, Sal."

"I should make a sign that says *Let Manny Play!*" Sal said. "I'll bring it to the game and make sure the coach sees it."

"Don't worry. If we play well today, I'll probably get in. If we can get a nice lead, the coaches will empty the bench."

Donald came by a few minutes later and they walked to the meeting area for the bus to Palisades. The day was cool and crisp, just right for football. Donald and Manny banged into each other all the way to the school, bumping their shoulder pads together and hearing the smack.

"I'm ready," Donald said. "Boy, am I ready. Running back, defense, wherever he plays me, I'm gonna make an impact this afternoon."

"Me, too," Manny said. "No more fooling around."

Coach Reynolds warned his team before the game not to take this opponent lightly. "They haven't won yet, but they've been close in every game," he said. "They'd like nothing more than to knock us off today. Let's not let it happen."

Hudson City took the opening kickoff for a short return and put the ball in play at its own 23-yard line. Coach had emphasized that the running game would be the key to this one, and they went right to work on it. Sure and steady, the Hornets drove up the field on a series of short runs, never breaking a long one but moving ahead. Fullback Jared Owen did much of the work.

DiMarco found Fiorelli for a nice gain over the middle, and then he scrambled around the end to get into Palisades' territory.

"We're moving the ball," Donald said. "Looking good."

Two more runs set up a first down at the Palisades' 30. DiMarco called signals and dropped back to pass, getting good protection from his linemen. Fiorelli was a step ahead of his defender, angling toward the middle of the field. DiMarco's pass was right on target, and Fiorelli hauled it in and sprinted into the end zone.

"Kickoff team, get out there!" the coach

shouted after DiMarco had kicked the extra point.

Manny looked at Donald. Donald just frowned. He hadn't played since that late kickoff in the second game.

Hudson City managed another touchdown toward the end of the second quarter, and the team trotted off the field with a 13–0 lead at the half.

"Excellent job," Coach Reynolds said at half-time. "Our offense is eating up a lot of time with the running game, and our defense has shut them down nicely. If we play smart, this game will be ours."

Manny looked intently at the coach. Maybe, if the team could get a couple of more scores, there'd be a chance for the second-stringers to play.

"We kick off to start the second half," Coach said. "I think we're ready to make a change. I've seen some good things in practice this week; some real improvements. Let's go back to our original kickoff team—the one that started the season. You guys remember what to do."

Manny pumped his fist and Donald smacked him on the arm.

"That's us," Donald said.

"No kidding," Manny answered.

"Let's kick some butt out there."

Manny nodded and felt a surge of energy. But it was more than just energy—it was confidence. No way would he mess up this opportunity.

The team trotted back to the field, but Manny could hardly control his excitement. He and Donald started bumping their shoulders together again, and Manny leaped high into the air as they reached the sideline.

"Let's crush 'em," he said to Donald.

"Everything we've got."

Manny looked up at the bleachers and saw Sal and his parents looking down. He gave a quick wave, then pointed at the field. Then he and Donald and nine other teammates ran onto the field, taking their places for the kickoff.

"Box and in," Manny said to Donald.

"Just like old times."

"No," Manny said, "a thousand times better."

Manny bounced in place a couple of times and stretched out his arms. Then he stood still as DiMarco got set to kick off.

As the kicker moved forward, Manny started to run, looking down the field to watch the flight of the ball. It soared through the air, coming down at about the 10-yard line, where the receiver caught it and started running.

Manny and Donald ran side by side, dodging blockers. The play was developing in the middle of the field, so Manny angled that way while Donald cut straight in from the sideline.

Hudson City players had converged on the play, slowing the ball carrier and forcing him toward the sideline. DiMarco had the runner in his grasp, and suddenly Manny was there, too, hitting him high and helping to bring him down.

Manny and DiMarco leaped up and slapped hands. "Nice hit," DiMarco said.

"Felt great," Manny said.

The impact had been sweet, with Manny's speed and momentum being just enough to stop the runner's progress. Donald put his arm around Manny's shoulder as they trotted off the field. "Awesome work, buddy," he said.

Coach Reynolds was clapping his hands as the kickoff team reached the sideline. "That's how it's done," he said. "That's the play we needed."

An assistant coach came over and patted Manny's helmet. "Good tackle," he said.

Manny turned toward the bleachers. Sal was jumping up and down and his parents were smiling, waving at Manny. Manny raised a fist in the air, then turned to watch the game.

Palisades had a different strategy for the second half, tossing a succession of short, quick passes that left Hudson City momentarily surprised. Palisades crossed midfield and continued to drive, gaining 6 or 7 yards each play.

The defense finally stiffened, with Anthony making consecutive tackles to leave Palisades with a third-and-eight at the Hudson City 24.

"Toughen up!" Manny yelled, feeling every bit a part of the action now. "Watch for that quick pass!"

The Palisades quarterback dropped back, looking toward the sideline. His favorite receiver was open, but the pass was wobbly and he had to back-track to get to the ball. That split second gave Fiorelli enough time to get there first, deflecting the ball just as the receiver reached it. The pass fell incomplete.

Fourth down. Too far for a field goal. Palisades tried another pass play, but the ball was over-thrown. Hudson City was back on offense.

With a two-touchdown lead, the Hornets played a ball-control offense, sticking with the running game that had worked so well in the first half. Jared Owen carried on four straight plays, moving the ball back into Palisades' territory. Then DiMarco found his favorite receiver, Jason Fiorelli, on a 25-yard pass over the middle.

That big pass play seemed to deflate the Palisades' defense. Owen took the next handoff straight up the middle and dashed into the sec-ondary, making a lightning-quick cut toward the sideline and running it in for a touchdown. DiMarco's kick made it 20–0, and Hudson City seemed headed for a certain victory.

"Our turn!" Manny said as the kickoff team took its place.

As the ball was kicked, Manny burst into high gear. A blocker was coming straight toward him, but Manny dodged right past him and zeroed in on the ball carrier, who was coming up his side of the field this time.

Both players were going full speed, and Manny braced for the impact. When they were 2 yards apart, Manny left his feet, driving his shoulder into the return man's waist and grabbing him with both arms.

Manny heard the *ooof!* as the runner took the blow and the *crack* as his pads hit the turf. But something else had happened: the ball had popped loose. Donald had it, and Manny scrambled to his feet as he watched his friend running toward the end zone.

Manny couldn't believe it. Donald was going to score! He was 5 yards ahead of his nearest pursuer and running at full stride. He crossed the 10-yard line, then the 5. Touchdown!

Manny tried to yell but he couldn't. He raced

over to Donald and grabbed him as Donald leaped into the air. The entire kickoff team was in the end zone now, shouting and swinging their fists.

Donald held the ball above his head and ran toward the sideline. The referee shouted at him to give up the ball, and Donald turned and tossed it over.

Teammates from the bench mobbed Donald. Coach Reynolds had come partway onto the field and put up a hand to stop Manny. "Great job, Manny!" he said. "Stay in there for the conversion. I told DiMarco what to call."

Manny ran back onto the field. The offense was huddled up near the goal line. DiMarco grabbed Manny's jersey and pulled him in.

"Remember that wingback pitch we ran in practice?" he said.

Manny nodded.

"We're running it now," DiMarco said. "Just follow me right over Anthony. Let's get you into the end zone."

Manny couldn't believe it. He'd made the big hit on the kickoff, and here was his reward. A chance to score. He gulped and took his position behind the tight end. His palms were sweaty, but he'd hold on to that ball.

DiMarco called signals and took the snap. Manny pivoted and grabbed the ball that was floating toward him. He cut into the line behind DiMarco. A defensive lineman had broken through, getting a hand on Manny's arm. Manny shook it off and squirted through the opening as players grunted and pushed and grabbed at him.

Beneath his feet he saw the goal line. Two defenders were on him, one hitting him high and the other low. Manny was going down, but it didn't matter. He was already in the end zone. He'd scored!

He heard the whistle blow and looked up, seeing the referee with his hands raised above his head. Two points!

Anthony grabbed Manny by the arms and pulled him to his feet, lifting him into the air. Teammates smacked his helmet and hooted. Manny felt tears in his eyes. This was more than he'd dreamed of.

The scoreboard changed from 26–0 to 28–0 as

Manny jogged up the field for the kickoff. Donald was racing across from the sideline and came flying into him, nearly knocking him to the ground.

"You're awesome, Manny!" Donald said. "We're awesome! Let's score another one. Right now!"

The Play of the Year

Manny sat on the living room couch with a bag of ice on his wrist. The injury was no big deal—he didn't even remember how it had happened—but Coach Reynolds had told him to ice it as a precaution. Sal sat right beside his older brother, looking at him in awe.

"That was the best game I ever saw, Manny," Sal said. "I couldn't believe it when you scored that touchdown."

Manny laughed. "It wasn't quite a touchdown, buddy. Just a two-point conversion."

"Just as good," Sal said. "Unbelievable. That was the play of the year!"

Dad grabbed Manny's shoulder and shook it gently. "I couldn't be prouder," he said. "You really were awesome this afternoon."

"Thanks," Manny said.

Hudson City had tacked on another touchdown and won the game, 34–0. Manny hadn't made any more tackles, but he and Donald did get in at linebacker for the closing series. All in all, it had been an incredible day.

The Giants were playing a late game today, taking on the Seahawks at four P.M. The family had gathered to watch the game, but most of their conversation was about the earlier game—the one in which Manny had emerged as a player.

Coach Reynolds had said after the game how proud he was of every player, especially the ones who'd taken advantage of the rare chance to play. "We've got a full team of reliable players now," he'd said. "There'll be plenty of playing time for everybody from here on out."

Most of the team planned to meet at McDonald's in the early evening, and this time Manny would be going. The coach had said they could even wear their game jerseys, as long as they promised not to get ketchup or mustard on them.

So after the Giants game, Manny put his jersey back on over his clothes. It was made of material that stretched to cover the shoulder pads, but it was still pretty huge without them. Manny didn't care. He didn't care, either, that the jersey was dirty. In fact, he was very proud of that dirt. If the jersey had still been clean, he wouldn't be going to McDonald's to hang out with the rest of the team.

"I won't be late," Manny said to his parents. "Just going to get a hamburger and a milk shake."

"You earned it," Mom said. "Go have a blast."

"I will."

"You're great, Manny!" shouted Sal.

"So are you, buddy."

Manny stepped out of the house and looked around. The sky was getting dark and there was a cool breeze. The maples were beginning to show traces of autumn color, but none of the leaves had fallen yet. There was still a long time left before winter. Still a lot of football games.

McDonald's was about six blocks from the house, near the edge of town. Manny started walking that way, toward the lights of the Boulevard. But he turned onto a side street and began to jog, still feeling a lot of energy, still wanting to move.

Here came that pitchout again, that moment of highlight-film intensity when Manny's whole universe was focused on the football. He grabbed it and cut toward the line, following DiMarco and Anthony, hearing the crashing of helmets and pads ahead of him, tearing loose from the grip of the defensive lineman.

And then the goal line beneath his feet, that hot-and-cold sensation in his gut that told him he'd scored, that the two points he'd put up on the scoreboard could never be erased. He'd done something big—bigger than he'd done in his whole, entire life. And this was only the beginning. Football, soccer, cross-country running. Whatever he chose to go after, he'd go after it in a big way.

Again he relived that play, again he felt that

surge of adrenaline and the satisfaction of a big-time effort. And then he was running down that field again, this time dodging blockers and zeroing in on the kickoff-return man, smacking him hard and jolting the football from his grasp.

Manny was sweating now; he'd run farther than he needed to. McDonald's was two blocks behind him and one block over. He didn't care. He raised his arms above his head and jogged in the middle of the nearly dark side street. He wiped his fore-head with his sleeve and smiled with the satisfac-tion of an athlete.

The breeze was blowing harder now, rustling the leaves above him as he ran. He wasn't ready for McDonald's just yet, wasn't ready to join his teammates. He needed a few more minutes alone, to feel his body moving, to make today's memories permanent.

He picked up his pace for a couple of blocks, opening his stride and running like a back in the open. He inhaled deeply and listened to the night, to the familiar hissing and whistling of the wind in the treetops. It sounded just right as he sprinted along the backstreet.

It sounded like a football stadium.

It sounded like "Manny!"

It sounded like the roar of the crowd.

* * *

Hudson City had cut the lead to one point. This defensive sequence would make the difference. "Stop 'em!" came Spencer's cry.

Half a minute remained. The ball came in to the Memorial center. He turned and faked to his left, but Jared had been watching that move all day. When the center pivoted to his right to shoot, Jared was ready. He leaped and blocked the shot, swatting it cleanly toward the sideline. Spencer got to it first, and Hudson City had a chance to win.

Spencer dribbled past midcourt and called Hudson City's final time-out.

"Get the ball inside," Coach Davis said in the huddle. He tapped Jared's chest with a finger. "We're putting this on you, Jared. You win this game for us. You do it."

Jared swallowed hard, but he wasn't nervous. He wanted that ball. *Let the guy grab me,* Jared thought. *Let him foul me, let him try to stop me. I'm going to score.*

"De-*fense*!" came the chant from the bleachers. "De-*fense*!"

And when the ball came to Jared, he did what he needed to do. Up and over his defender, who pushed back and grunted, leaving his feet and reaching toward the backboard. Jared's shot was clean and sure, drifting above his opponent's hands and into the basket. Hudson City was back in the lead.

Memorial frantically brought the ball up with the seconds ticking away. A long shot at the buzzer fell short. The spectators were suddenly silent.

Jared pumped his fist and hugged Spencer. Hudson City was back in business.

"That's it. That's the Hudson City way," said Fiorelli as they walked off the court. "They're like, 'We'll stuff these guys. We can hold and foul and talk trash all day,' and we're like, 'Talk all you want. We'll put it right back in your face.'"

Fiorelli turned to Jared and gave him a hard high five. "That's right, *Mr. T!*" he said. "You! You! You! You showed 'em. You did."

Jared didn't say anything. He just smiled broadly and shook his coach's hand as the team made its way to the bus.

* * *

RICH WALLACE

was a high school and college athlete and then a sportswriter before he began writing novels. He is the author of many critically acclaimed sports-themed novels, including *Wrestling Sturbridge, Shots on Goal,* and *Restless: A Ghost's Story.* Wallace lives with his wife and teenage sons in Honesdale, Pennsylvania.